# K

## is for
## Kitten

Niki Clark Leopold

illustrated by

**Susan Jeffers**

G. P. Putnam's Sons · New York

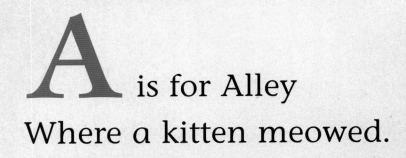

# A is for Alley
Where a kitten meowed.

Finally I found her,
Tiny and loud.

# B is for Brave.
All the way home
She purred in my arms,
Soft fur and bones.

# C is for Cream

And comfort and cozy.

She lapped it all up;

I named her Miss Rosie.

D is for Dog.

Amos is jealous.

Can they be friends?

The morning will tell us.

**E** is for Eyes
To see through the grass,
Chase a gray squirrel.
Rosie's so fast!

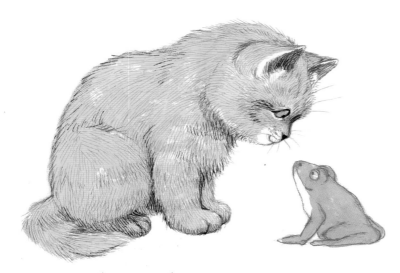

**F** is for Frog

Who hops by in a blur.

Rosie's surprised—

Up goes her fur!

# G's for the Gerbil
All in a tizzy,

Spinning his wheel—
Rosie is dizzy.

# H is for Hiss.
## The sprinkler turns on.

Rosie's upset—
"Hiss!" and she's gone.

# I is for Insects: Beetles and ants.

Crickets and katydids—Look at them dance.

# J is for Jump

Onto a sack,

Over a barrel

To Amos's back.

**K** is for Kitten,
So silly, so smart,
Face like a pansy—
Jump into my heart.

# L is for Lick.
Perched on the rail,
She washes herself
From whiskers to tail.

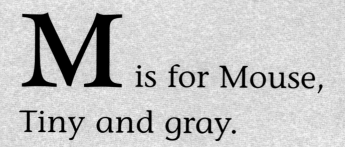

**M** is for Mouse,
Tiny and gray.

You frighten Miss Rosie,
She slinks away.

# N is for Nap.
Curled in the shade,

She's dreaming of goldfish,
And I, lemonade.

# O is for Oops!
Rosie's out on a limb.
Mama Robin is mad—
In trouble again!

$P$ is for Pond.
I don't think she's met
That face in the water.
Now Rosie's all wet!

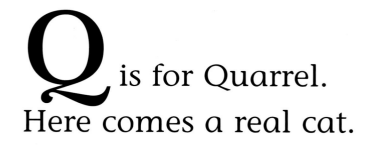

Q is for Quarrel.
Here comes a real cat.

"This is *my* garden,"
Says Rosie, "you scat!"

# R's for Rambunctious:

Chasing her tail,
Batting a bee,
Upsetting the pail.

**S** is for Shadow.
Wherever she goes,
A little gray kitten
Plays with her toes.

# T is a Tiger.
Rosie pretends
To prowl in the jungle
With monkeys for friends.

# U is for Up.

What a view of the town!

Roofs and a river—

But how to get down?

# V

is for Vet,
Who pets Rosie's chin,
Saying, "Fatten her up.
She's a little too thin."

# W's Whiskers

Dripping with cream.

Mice and men have them, but
Hers are supreme!

# X is for eXtra.
## If cats have nine lives,

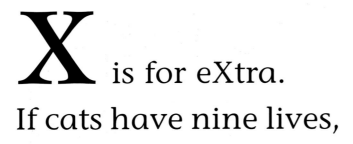

 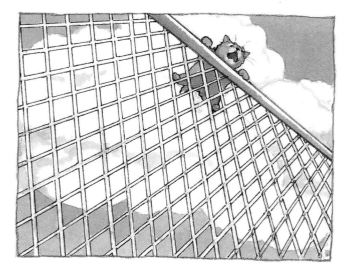

Miss Rosie has ten—
She knows it inside.

# Y is for Yawn.
My lost-and-found cat . . .
It's been a full day,
Climb into my lap.

# Z is for ZZzz's. Z Z z z Z Z z z ᶻᶻᶻᶻ

With love all around her,
Rosie is dozing.
I'm so glad I found her!

For all the cats who've jumped into my heart!
—N. C. L.

For Pam Gockley,
devoted friend of creatures great and small.
—S. J.

Published simultaneously in Canada. Printed in Hong Kong by South China Printing Co. (1988) Ltd. Designed by Gina DiMassi. Text set in Stone Informal. The art was prepared in gouache and colored inks on watercolor paper.   Library of Congress Cataloging-in-Publication Data  Leopold, Nikia Speliakos Clark.   K is for kitten / Niki Clark Leopold ; illustrated by Susan Jeffers.  p. cm.  Summary: A rhyming alphabet book which follows a kitten named Rosie from the alley in which she is found to the "ZZzzs" she enjoys with the family that gives her a home.   1. Cats—Juvenile poetry. 2. Children's poetry, American. 3. Alphabet rhymes. [1. Cats—Poetry. 2. American poetry. 3. Alphabet.] I. Jeffers, Susan, ill. II. Title.  PS3612.E38 K14 2002  811'.6—dc21 2001048252  ISBN 0-399-23563-9
1 3 5 7 9 10 8 6 4 2
FIRST IMPRESSION